The Peacock and the Crow

From an old Chinese fable

Published by Four Winds Press
A Division of Scholastic Magazines, Inc., New York, N.Y.

Printed in the United States of America.
Library of Congress Catalogue Card Number: 70-81693

The Peacock and the Crow

written and illustrated by
ANN KIRN

FOUR WINDS PRESS · NEW YORK

to
KIM

One spring morning, Peacock and Crow strolled through a bamboo and plum thicket.

They met Lord Tiger looking handsome in his tawny coat with its black stripes.

"Good morning, Lord Tiger," they greeted him.

"Good morning, Peacock. Good morning, Crow," said Lord Tiger returning their greetings.

"Tomorrow is my wedding day. I should like for the two of you to attend."

"Thank you, Lord Tiger, we shall be happy to," answered the two friends.

They walked on to the winding meadow river.

Crow looked at Peacock, who was dull yellow like an old hen. Then he looked down at his own plain white feathers.

"How shall we adorn ourselves for Lord Tiger's wedding?" he asked.

"Yes, we do look rather plain," said Peacock. "Let's get up early tomorrow and gather flowers to cover our dull feathers."

And they both went home to spend the night.

The next morning they gathered meadow flowers. They gathered blue and yellow and white flowers.

They tucked the beautiful flowers among their tail feathers, then up their backs and on their wings.

Finally they were all covered. Crow tucked a daisy on top of his head, and Peacock put two blue corn-flowers on his.

"You look very gay," said Crow.
Peacock looked at himself reflected in the water.
"Yes, I do," he said, "and so do you."

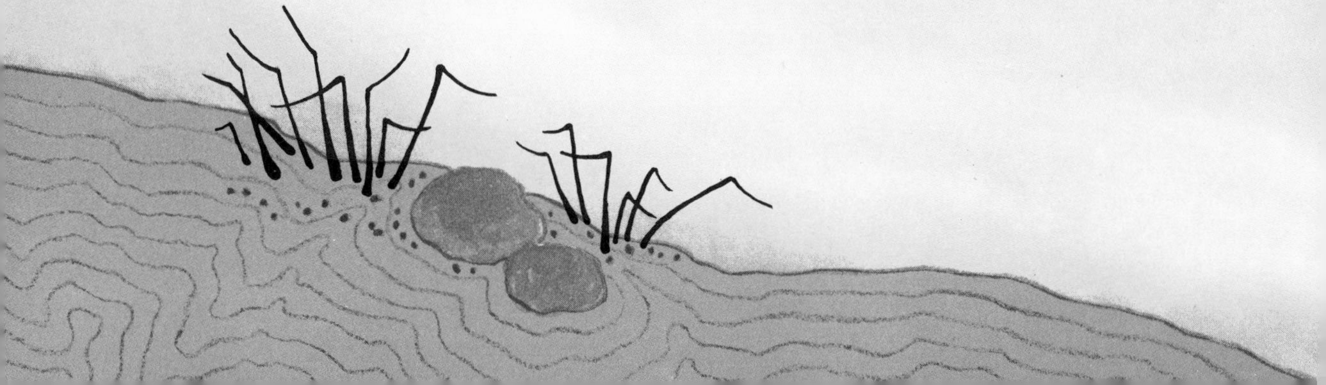

They strutted proudly down the path toward Lord Tiger's home.

But with every step they lost one flower. Two flowers. Then another. And another.

When they turned to look behind them, they saw a trail of the brightly colored flowers.

Looking at each other they squawked, "What shall we do? What shall we do? We look as plain as old hens!"

"I have an idea," said Crow.

"Tell me quick," said Peacock, "for I am ashamed to attend handsome Lord Tiger's wedding in these dull feathers."

"The King of Annan is having a moon-gazing house built on down the river," replied Crow. "I saw it this morning as I flew over to meet you."

"How can King Annan's house help us?" asked Peacock crossly.

"Oh, it is a wonderful house. The railings on the porch are being decorated with dragons. They are painted blue and yellow and green. The workmen should soon go to eat their lunch. We can hurry over and get their pots of paint."

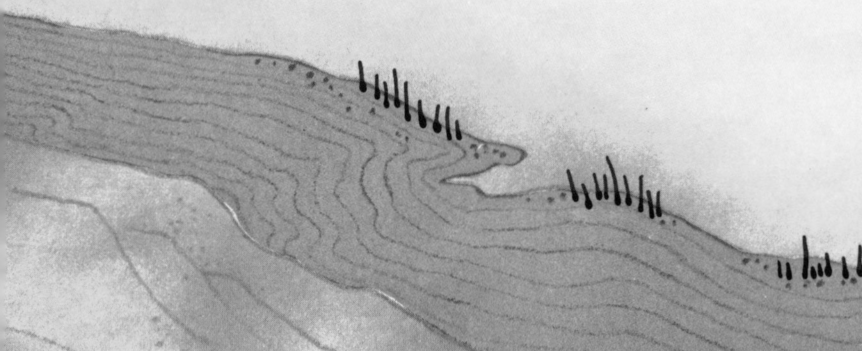

They brought the paint pots back with them.

"This is your idea," said Peacock, "so you should paint me first."

Crow held the paint brush in his strong beak. He painted moons of yellow and blue on Peacock's tail feathers. Then he decorated the rest of his feathers with beautiful greens, blues, and yellows.

"There you are," he said as he finished. "You look fancy enough for a King's wedding, as well as Lord Tiger's."

Peacock stood up straight. He stretched out his long slender neck and spread out his tail to dry the painted feathers.

He looked magnificent.

When he saw himself reflected in the water, he cackled, "Kwong-toh! Kwong-toh! How beautiful I am! How very beautiful I am!"

And he strutted up and down the river bank with his tail spread in a big fan, although his feathers were quite dry.

Crow called to him, "Friend, it is your turn to paint me. Come show how good an artist you are!"

But Peacock was proud and jealous. He didn't want Crow to be as handsome as he for Lord Tiger's wedding.

So he cunningly said, "Didn't you hear the cry of that eagle? We must fly! We must hide ourselves!"

And pretending to hurry, he ran into the pots of paint and knocked them into the river.

"I didn't hear an eagle cry," said Crow.

"Oh, I must have been mistaken," said Peacock. "Come I will paint you."

"The paint is at the bottom of the river," croaked Crow.

"But here is one pot."

"Then hurry."

Peacock picked up the brush with his bill and painted very rapidly.

"There!" he cried. "You look lovely!"

Crow ran to look at himself in the water.

He saw that his feathers had been painted black from the top of his head to the tip of his tail. He opened his beak to fuss at tricky Peacock.

His voice choked in his throat, and he could only scream harshly, "Caw! Caw!"

Ever since then crows have been black and have had a very harsh voice.

But Crow now knows that when the sunlight strikes his glossy feathers, they shine every color of the rainbow.

Peacocks are handsome with their bright colors. But their voices sound no better, as they proudly screech, "Kwong-toh! Kwong-toh!"

And all birds know that a proud peacock is a false friend.